DECODING ZINDAGI

SHUBHAM DUMBRE

ISBN 979-888569471-1

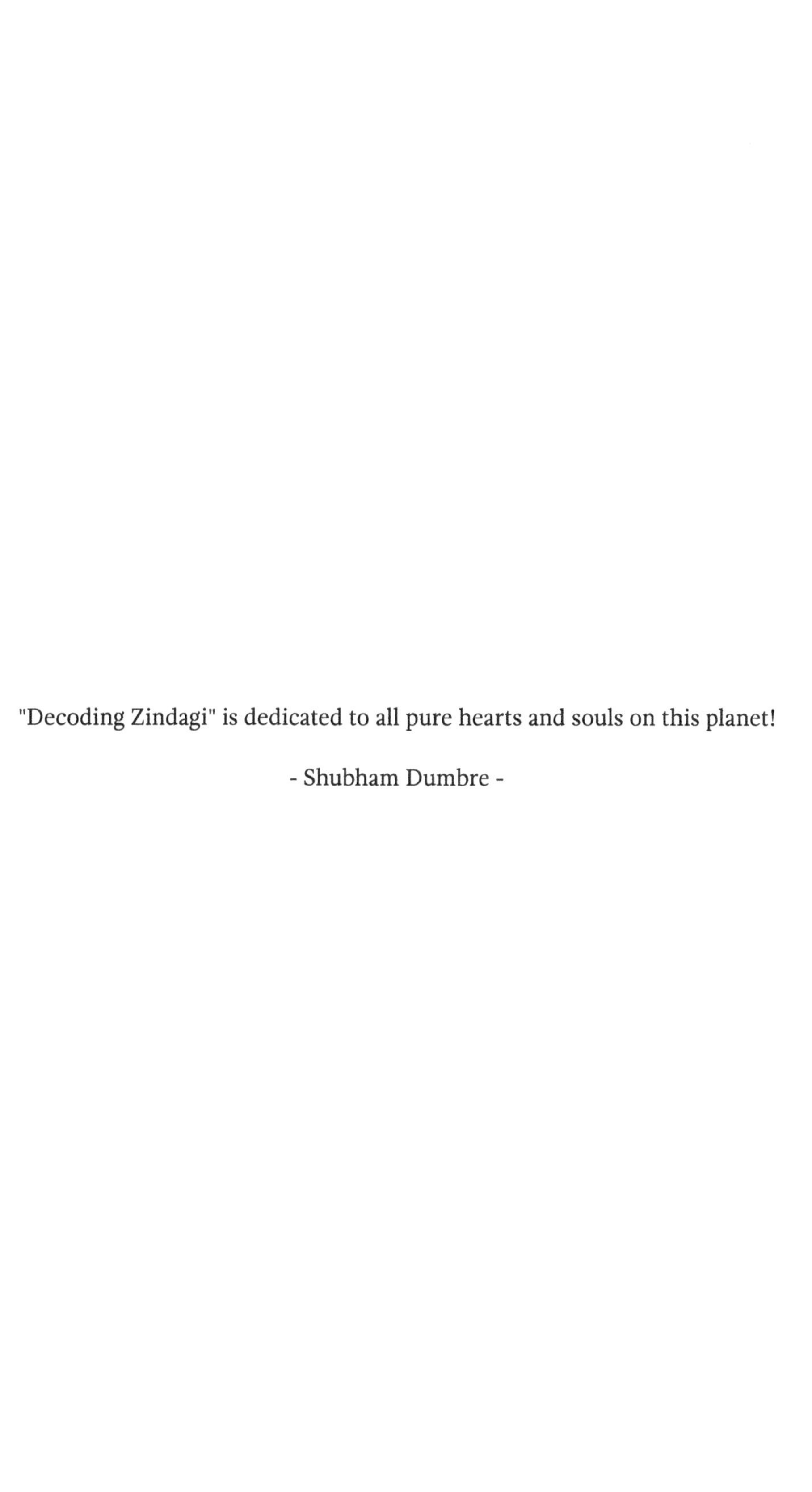

"Decoding Zindagi" is dedicated to all pure hearts and souls on this planet!

- Shubham Dumbre -

Contents

Foreword

"A journey of a thousand miles, begins with a single step!"

This line is suitable enough to define Er. Shubham Mangesh Dumbre, a gentleman, an entrepreneur, a technologist who happens to be my elder brother.

He's a person who keeps on trying new challenging ideas, consistently learns from his experiments, adapts and improvises his actions strategically. This book is an addition to his result driven energy, passion, dedication, persistence and creativity. For me he is a true artist, for whom I can vouch for. Hc is my catalyst!

I'm fortunate enough to be an Executive Editor of "**Decoding Zindagi**". Brother, you were a fantastic Executive Editor for my book "**All About Life**"... and this time, our roles are swapped! I'm happy with my promotion! All the best for this new dimension of your life brother, I wish you all the luck and success ahead!

Readers, I personally recommend you to read this book as it has an unusual, realistic perspective towards usual aspects and emotions of our lives. You will definitely enjoy "**Decoding Zindagi**". We look forward to your feedbacks!

Thank You!

- Ms. Mansi Mangesh Dumbre
(Founder, MD Creations)

Acknowledgements

This book is officially published by Delta The Innovators (DTI)

www.deltatheinnovators.com

"We are innovators, who regularly work hard and smart to create an alchemy of marvelous products, operational excellence and pioneering customer services by empowering talents with eternal opportunities to discover their best, right from their nascent stage.

We believe in simplifying things by gaining all sorts of challenging experiences and by coming up with quality results that will benefit the world."

DTI is a stalwart philanthropic syndicate that has firmly impacted more than 10000+ people by imparting education and by providing innovative technical solutions regularly.

Preface

About Shubham Dumbre (Founder, Delta The Innovators):

- **LinkedIn Profile**: www.linkedin.com/in/ishubhamdumbre
- **Personal Website**: www.ishubhamdumbre.home.blog
- **Instagram Profile**: www.instagram.com/ishubhamdumbre_
- **Facebook Profile**: www.facebook.com/ishubhamdumbre
- **Email ID**: ishubhamdumbre@gmail.com
- **Official Website**: www.deltatheinnovators.com
- **YouTube**: www.youtube.com/c/deltatheinnovators

• • •

First Impression 2022

• • •

Prologue

The function of a man is to live and not just to exist! Certainty is of course, scarce and expensive.

ABCD of Life: Our life depends on our Actions (A), starts with our Birth (B), exists because of our Choices (C) and ends with our Death (D).

We are never stronger than tested, as circumstances build a man. There is always a room for improvisation and sometimes, life brings us to a point, to make a point. So, life is not just what happens to us, it is we, who make life happen!

Truth is definitely stranger than fiction. The hardest choices require the finest wills, discipline, consistency, persistence, courage and a bunch of sacrifices. One has to be at the right place, at the right time, with a right set of people, to lead an ideal life ahead!

We cannot bring back the ones who are already lost, but we can happily live with the ones who exist and actually matter to us. Believe me, I trust you to do what needs to be done, and for now, let's together deep dive into "**Decoding Zindagi**".

I've written this edition, to present and express a handful of facts that impact us, shape us and our lives altogether. Some among these are master keys of life. Our thoughts, experiences, challenges and time impact our choices, actions, decisions and life.

This is not a regular novel or script. Every chapter has two distinctions, each loaded with fresh original content. It is a tricky combination of simple English with relevant examples and poetic wordplays in Hindi language.

I hope you enjoy this word treat!

CHAPTER I

Today

Right now, we all are in our Today, and so, I genuinely feel, that the word Today, does not require any special introduction or technical definition.

Present tense is specifically generalized using the word today, and so, we can smartly frame it as "Future is a Present that we get from our Past!"

Our today is full of various activities! With every passing moment, we do, what we are meant to do, and sometimes, we even do what we are not meant to do!

Right from some regular tasks that we do, to the different activities that we carry out, our today has 'n' number of variations daily. Still, there are some common things in almost everyone's Today, like travelling, talking, eating, working, etc.

My main motive to elaborate on this topic is to explore Today from its critical perspectives, as it will help us to assess our present, and its realistic nature, depending upon our actions and associated reactions.

Here I present before you, a wordplay from my end, simplifying Today!

"Kal, aaj aur kal,
Ki baat hi kuch aur hain!
Jo aaj ho raha hain,
Vo kal ho chuka hoga,
Aur jo kal hona hain,
Vo aaj ke baad ho jaayega!

Jo kal beet chuka hain,
Vo phir se aayega toh nahi,
Aur jo aaj beet raha hain,
Vo kal phir milega nahi!

Beeti hui baaton ko hi,
Agar tum yaad karte rahoge,
Toh aaj poori tarah,
Jiyoge kaise?
Aane waale kal ki hi,
Agar tum chinta karte rahoge,
Toh aaj poori tarah,
Jiyoge kaise?

Aaj jo saath hain,
Vo shayad kal tumhein
Poochenge bhi nahi!
Aur jo kal saath honge,
Vo shayad aaj tumhein,
Jaante bhi nahi!
Jo beete hue kal mein thee,
Vo aane waale kal mein honge hi,
Aisa zaroori bhi toh nahi!

Waqt ke aagaaz se,
Aaj ki apni ek alag pehachan rahi hain!
Kai saaron ka aaj, kal bann gaya hain!
Aur kai saaron ka kal, aaj bann chuka hain!

Bas fark itna hain,
Ki kaun aaj ji raha hain,
Aur kaun
Beete ya aane waale kal mein khoya hain!

Jo pehle ki hui galtiyon se seekh kar,
Aaj ubhar raha hain,
Uska aane waala kal hi,
Uski zindagi ka hal hain!

Jo aage hone waali galtiyon ko samajhkar,
Aaj sambhal raha hain,
Uske beete hue kal mein bhi,

Uski zindagi ka hal hain!

Aaj ki apni ek alag si khaasiyat hain...
'Aa' aane waale waqt ki dastak deta hain, aur 'j', jaane waale waqt ki!"

On this precious note, I would like to take your leave for Today, have got to reach somewhere now! I hope, you all have decoded the right essence from our above synergy!

CHAPTER II

Beauty

"Baat nazar ki nahi...nazariye ki hoti hain!
Khoobsurat toh gulaab bhi hota hain...
Par vo bhi...kaanto se bhara hota hain!"

Beauty is something that we all admire, and trust me, even if we specify that men are handsome and women are beautiful, here, in this particular word piece, the word 'Beauty' signifies and applies to both men and women.

Many a times, we hear people saying - "Our inner beauty matters more, than our outer appearance."

Yes of course, that is true, but then, what exactly is this 'Inner Beauty'? Can we see it? Can we feel it?

Yeah, it can be seen and felt...only if we possess that eye, that sight to detect it, feel it, find it and retain it!

Now another question arises, how to get or develop that eye, that sight needed here? For that, we need to specifically change our perspective, our mindset towards people, as that is a unique way, to attain it.

Beauty not only means how you look, but actually means, how you are seen by everyone around. Beauty hardly counts what you wear, it focuses on your clothes of character, dignity, and behaviour. 'Manners' make a person even more beautiful and 'Attitude' towards life, either positive or negative, plays an important role in increasing or decreasing beauty at every stage of life. A person's nature, lifestyle, etc. are the factors that count here proportionately.

"Perfection is beauty, but beauty is not always perfection!" - this applies in our lives...even in the smallest slice of moments. It is not just because something or someone is perfect, it is beautiful, or vice versa, but because it is beautiful, it should be the best, tending towards perfection.

Here comes my next wordplay, this time on “Beauty” -

Maine Quaynaat se poocha..
"Khoobsurti kya hain? Kahan hain...?
Waadon mein? Iradon mein? Ya Jasbaaton mein?
Lafzon mein? Alfaazon mein? Ya Yaadon mein?
Mohabatt mein? Nafrat mein? Ya Junooniyat mein?
Ibadat mein? Shahadat mein? Ya Ganimiyat mein?"

Quaynaat kuch na boli...
Hawa ki baahon mein,
Patton sang vo doli...
Mehasoos hua...
Jaise kuch kehna chah rahi hain...
Vo sarsaraati tehaniyaan...
Vo pyari si titliyaan...
Unn behati leharon sang...,
Jinko nahi tha gumaan...
Sab kuch baha le jaane ka...
Bin kuch bole,
Sab kuch keh jaane ka...!

Yeh khsitij mann ko bhaa gaya...
Dil ko bhi rula gaya!
Aur apni aakhein band kar...
Maine khoobsurti kya hain...
Kaha hain...
Sahi maaino mein jaan li!

Kya aap jaanna chhahoge mujhe kya jawaab aaya tha?

Khoobsurti wahi hain aur khoobsurti wohi hain...
Jismein tu...
Aur tera jahaan hain!

That’s all for this one from my side mates! I hope you all got my words, and felt their beauty!

CHAPTER III

Love

Love is a topic that needs no special introduction, as we all are familiar with it, since our inception! We all are connected to it and have witnessed its supreme power. Love is experienced by everyone, and it exists for both the alive and the deceased!

As per my understanding -
"Rishte alag hote hain...mohabatt toh saari ek hi hoti hain!"

'Love' is simply complicated. Some call it a sacrifice, some name it as a lifelong partnership, for some, it is a divine bond, commitment and what not! Love cannot be sold or bought, neither can it be stored.

According to me, Love is affection, a timeless bond that nurtures with time, care and dedication. It has many different forms of expression. Generally it is positive, at times negative, sometimes one sided, etc.

'Life' and 'Love' go hand in hand, even if one's story completes or remains incomplete! The 'if' in 'life' when is bestowed by 'ov' in 'love', everything in this universe, seems to be magnanimous!

Every year, we celebrate the Valentine's Day, actually the Valentine's Week, a time when people think that love can be celebrated with teddies, chocolates, hugs, promises, etc. But my simple question for all is, why are we bound to this? Why do we think, that love can only be celebrated in this particular week? Is only a week sufficient to express love, live love? Think about it!

Lust is not Love! Also, sudden attraction is not love! Love is something that happens itself...and has its own unique flavour, for each one who experiences it. We all are aware of some famous lovers and their epic lovestories, which include the Radha-Krishna, Romeo-Juliet, Jodhaa-Akbar, Majnu-Laila, etc. Each one of these, is just amazing in its own aura. Shah Jahan's love for his queen Mumtaz is alive even today in the form of Taj

Mahal.

'Perfect Love' is an ideal concept that does not exist in this world! There are always some strengths and weaknesses in love, then might it be any bond that we consider! Generally, opposites attract, and become successful lovers. But this doesn't mean like ones repel each other always, as love has its magic everywhere.

A mother's love for her child, a father's love for his children, a family's love for its relatives, a singer's love for his/her voice, a dancer's love for his/her steps, a tailor's love for threads, investigators love for proofs, etc. are some notable examples of Love.

Love exists between living beings, and their bonds with the living and nonliving things! I love my mobile phone and laptop too. Love is a healthy combination of trust and care. If you're an animal lover, and you possess a pet, say a kitten or a labrador, you already know what care is...what love is! My perspective towards love says -

"Vo zindagi, zindagi nahi,
Jismein pyar nahi...!

Vo kahani ka antt nahi,
Jismein pyar nahi...!

Vo kahani adhuri hi rahi...
Jismein pyar nahi...!

Aur pyar baya karne, jatane ke liye...
Chaand-taaron ki bhi koi zaroorat nahi...

Kyunki agar sachha pyar hain...
Toh vo pyar kabhi marega nahi...

Dilon se dilon ki bewafaai,
Vo kabhi karega nahi!"

Love happens easily, but the challenge that lovers have to accomplish, is the challenge of retaining it forever! True lovers survive in any situation, difficult times, shortcomings and consequences together. And yes, here ultimately, what matters the most is 'Trust', 'Understanding' and 'Maturity' in bonds. Time plays a crucial role in every such case here.

That's all from my side for now, as we can go on and on. Hope you loved it!

CHAPTER IV

Humanity

All the people in our world, thought of as a group, is the primary definition of the noun humanity. Another meaning suggests that the quality of being kind and understanding, is humanity.

Let's coin it in our words, our way. Humanity is something that actually defines humans, our nature, actions and responsiveness! It differentiates humans from other living and non-living beings. Thus, humanity is a key to the human nature and levels of humanity talk about a person's overall character.

Many a times we come across some social media posts in opposition of child or animal abuse, and the most interesting part about such posts is that these instantly trigger our humanity levels, our tolerance levels. Such incidents force us think about human virtues and vices.

Whenever we face any calamity or disaster, we humans tend to help each other, even if we are strangers. This is just because humanity binds us to do so. Helping the poor ones, by either giving them food, clothes, utilities or shelter, etc. is humanity. So, humanity is synonymous to help!

Here are my thoughts on humanity and its related phenomenon -

Insaaniyat kya hain?
Kya vo kahin milti hain?
Kya vo kahin ugti hain?
Kya vo kahin dikhti hain?
Kya vo kahin rukti hain?

Aise kai saare saawalon ke jawaab,
Insaaniyat mein hi hain!

Nahi samjhe?
Koi baat nahi!

Aao saath milkar,
Iss paheli ko sulzhaaye!

Pehala sawaal tha,
"Kya insaaniyat kahin milti hain?"
Iska hal insaan ke insaan hone mein hain!

Doosra sawaal tha,
"Kya insaaniyat kahin ugti hain?"
Iska asal jawaab,
Har insaan ne sabke saath ugaai,
Apni rishton ki fasal hain!

Teesra sawaal tha,
"Kya insaaniyat kahin dikhti hain?"
Iska jawaab nazar,
Aur nazariye mein chupa hain!

Aur aakhri sawaal tha,
"Kya insaaniyat kahin rukti hain?"
Sach kahoon toh,
Iska jawaab hi aise saare sawaalon ka uttar hain,
Iss poori paheli ka hal hain!

Jaanna nahi chhahoge vo jawaab kya hain?

Waise ek baat bata doon,
Ki iska hal,
Maine har sawaal mein diya hain!

Sahi samjha aapne,
Iss paheli ka hal hain -
"Insaaniyat"!

Har insaan ki niyat hi,
Inn saare sawaalon ka hona hain,
Aur sulazhna bhi!
Khudgarz insaan,

Insaaniyat ke maaino ko todta hain,
Marodta hain,
Toh wahi niswaarth manushya,
Dusron ki bhalaai ke liye,
Agrasar hota hain!

Isi ke saath,
Hum sabhi ne ye samjha hain,
Ki maanavta hi ekmaatra dharma hain!
Insaaniyat hi sahi maaino mein,
Sachha karma hain!

Life is a precious gift to us, but not for all, as not everyone is as lucky as us, to live it our way! Crimes challenge humanity, then might it be a terrorist attack, or something else worse like that! Organ donation is something, that is truly appreciated, as it favours humanity! Humanity is hope. Helping all living beings, to live their lives according to their standards, choices, and freedom is humanity!

We've frequently heard and come across a popular saying,
"Service to Man, is Service to God".

Now atheists who are reading this word piece, please don't complain that you don't believe in the idea of God! Humanity is all about humans, our beliefs, our actions and bonds. We all know that, we all are humans and before belonging to any religion, we are all bound to humanity.

Humanity is not about complaining or fighting,
It's about solving and making our way out of those!

Humanity is not about selfish gains,
But about understanding, and helping others overcome their pains.

And ultimately,
It's all karma!
Whatever we do,
Comes back to us,
In some manner or the other!

So, it entirely depends on us,
What we want for us,
And what we'll actually get for ourselves,
From whatever we do!

With this, I would like to conclude this topic Humanity!

CHAPTER V

Stalking

An unknown or an indirectly known surveillance on someone, by someone is known as stalking.

Stalking behaviours are interrelated to harassment and intimidation and may include following the victim in person or monitoring them. It is a criminal offense, as prying is a form of investigation, and here, it is an unofficial intervention. Mostly it has been observed that females are victims of stalking, but there are also other forms of stalking including spying, cyber bullying, etc.

In our so-called modern technological world, we have cameras, microphones, technology etc. everywhere surrounding us. Are we sure, that it is working only for us and our comforts, as per our will? Are we sure enough to say that no one except us is using them? We never know, who is monitoring us through that webcam/front camera, which is just on our handsets and laptops. We're unsure whether our microphone is muted or is it bugging us! We don't even know, who is stalking and tracking us, our activities, our behaviour and our actions, along with our transactions!

Previously, stalking was limited, as it was in person but now, online stalking, better known as cyber stalking, has spread across the globe. Internet and smart electronic devices are used to stalk and harass individuals, groups, or organizations. It may include false accusations, defamation, slander and libel along with monitoring, identity theft, threats, vandalism, solicitation for sex, or gathering information that may be used to threaten, embarrass or harass. Offline stalking and cyber stalking go hand in hand, as there's a real and a virtual collision here.

Stalkers can be both, harmful and risky! They use overt and covert intimidation, threats and violence to frighten their victims. A form of mental assault in which the perpetrator repeatedly, unwantedly, and disruptively breaks into the life-world of their known or unknown target, in order to gain something from it or harm it, can be a simpler understandable explanation of stalking.

Section 354D Indian Penal Code 1860 (IPC) states that -
"A man following or contacting a woman, despite clear indication of disinterest by the woman, or monitoring her use of the internet or electronic communication is stalking. A man committing the offence of stalking would be liable for imprisonment up to three years for the first offence, and shall also be liable to fine and for any subsequent conviction would be liable for imprisonment up to five years and with fine."

Now, the question that stands before us is, can stalking be eliminated? If yes, then how? If no, then why? We ourselves directly or indirectly stalk people, especially women, in some manner or the other! This includes our online activities, social interactions, those 'n' number of comparisons that we make, while looking or analysing something and someone. Our mind reciprocates, makes us think a lot! Also, we all being different from each other, in various terms including ideologies and stabilities, have varied reactions and plans alternatively. Admiring someone and stalking someone are two completely different concepts, but most of us don't even know about it!

Stalking is wrong, and we humans tend to do wrong things more than the right ones! Here's my attempt to present it in a rhetoric form -

Chup chup kar kitna dekhoge?
Bhoolo nahi,
Tumhein bhi koi,
Tumhari hi tarah,
Dekh raha hain!

Jal jal kar kitna dekhoge?
Yaad rakhna,
Tumse bhi koi,
Tumhari hi tarah,
Jal raha hain!

Tum jise dekh rahe ho,
Vo anjaana ya anjaani,

Kisi baat se,
Yaa toh koi rishta rakhte honge,
Ya phir unse
Tumhara koi naata hi nahi hoga!

Ho sakhta hain,
Tumhare mansoobe,
Uss anjaane ya anjaani ke liye,
Bhayanak ho, jaanleva ho!

Par ek baat ko samajh lo,
'Jaisi karni, vaisi bharni!'
Kisi ki zindagi mein,
Uski marzi ke bina dakhl dena,
Ruh ka apraadh hain!

Kisi bhi stree ko,
Buri drishti se dekhne waalon,
Mahabharat, Ramayan aur
Baaki mahagaathaon se waakif nahi ho kya?

Har jeev ka sammaan,
Zaroori hain!
Mukkhyataha,
Stree ka sammaan,
Sarvadhik mahattvapurna hain!

Sammaan yaane adhikaar,
Aur adhikaar matlab aatmanirbharta!

Bure kaam karne mein maza zaroor aata hoga,
Par unka anjaam,
Bhi bura hi hota hain!

Ab yeh hum par nirbhar karta hain,
Ki hum iss 'stalking' ki bimaari ka ilaaj,
Kaise karte hain!
Iska ilaaj hi,

Hamare samaj ka aur
Hamara vikas hain!

With this, I would like to wind up this topic here at this point! I hope, you got my take over it!

CHAPTER VI

Choices

At some or the other point, we all have answered many true/false, yes/no, right/wrong type of questions and problems in our lives! As the head and tail of a coin can never be on the same side, two opposite shores of a sea, even after being connected, cannot be on a single side, similarly, there are at least two possibilities in any situation.

Boundaries play a pivotal role in most of the cases, and we are able to either select or reject, on the basis of experiences, reviews, choices, options, opinions and paths that arc availablc in rcality.

We select what we like, and we reject what we don't! This can be summed up as a 'Choice'!

Life is too short to do everything, and so, if you're aspiring to do everything that you come across and what comes across you, then please note, that's not feasible. Our comfort zone and priorities brutally kill ambitions, leak the dedication that we possess! So, our choices need to be smart and organised.

MCQ's i.e., Multiple Choice Questions are an integral part of our examinations. Have we ever thought, why is it so? The solution to this query is decisions, and the power associated with it is the decision-making power! They make us answer MCQ's, to check and develop our problem-solving skills, decision making and breaking powers! Decision breaking powers refer to the application of one's decisions over others decisions, either due to superiority or control. Therefore, our decisions play a key role in shaping our lives, motives and characters!

I've analysed a truth of life after my deep study on and over it. My analysis concluded -
"If everything is right, there is something wrong,
and if everything is wrong, there is something right!"

To understand this important truth, you'll need to have your perspective, your realistic point of view towards life. Somehow, we all are connected and associated, and so our choices and decisions impact all our connections and network, either directly or indirectly, depending upon the type of bond we have, share, develop and nurture with them.

We all know that if we consume a lot of sugar daily, we'll soon be diabetic! Similarly, if we respond positive every time, we'll soon face many problems! Multitasking is a myth, and so, please don't expect me, to accept it! One cannot do everything all at once! Therefore, it can never be a 'Yes' all the time. There has to be a 'No', in order to strike a balance between both of them. Repulsion is critical for striking a healthy balance among our choices.

One who looks at the background from all directions, has his/her eyes ahead in time, knows or predicts major consequences of his/her decisions and choices will always choose wisely between a Yes and a No! Selection and Rejection definitely affect, rather impact us, and so, not always a Yes, but even a No matters, many a times!

Here comes our fresh word cake for this one -

"Hum hamesha sahi nahi ho sakhte,
Aur na hi hum hamesha galat hote hain!
Saara waqt ka khel hain!

Kai baar, kuch paane ke liye,
Kuch khona padta hain...
Aur vo kuch khone par,
Rona bhi padta hain!

Phir chhahe tum chupkar ro lo,
Ya duniya ko dikhakar,
Kuch maaine nahi rakhta hain!

Kisi ne ekdum sahi kaha hain –
Tum sabko khush nahi rakh sakhte!
Tum sabko khush nahi kar sakhte!

Koi na koi, hamari

Kisi na kisi baat se,
Naaraz, khafa ya gussa,
Ho hi jaata hain!
Aur jaane anjaane mein,
Hum bhi aisa hi karte hain!

Kyun hum yeh bhool jaate hain,
Ki agar kuch hamare kahe mutabik na hua ho,
Toh uske peeche bhi koi wajah rahi hogi!

Kyun hume yeh yaad nahi rehata,
Ki har koi alag hain, bhinn hain,
Sabhi ki paristhitiyaan alag hain...
Toh sabke nirnay,
Samaan kaise honge?

Sahi ya galat ka chunaav,
Hum khud karte hain!
Apni manzoori ya naa-manzoori bhi,
Hum swayam darshaate hain!

Aur isse yeh tatthya saaf ho jaata hain,
Ki hamesha Haa sahi nahi hota,
Aur Naa galat nahi hota hain!

Neeti, paristhiti, samay aur maansikta par,
Haa ya Naa,
Nirbhar karta hain!

Aur ha, yaad rakhna,
Kai dafa, Haa se zyada,
Naa zaroori hota hain!"

Learn to say a NO, whenever and wherever necessary! Choose and decide wisely!

CHAPTER VII

Vacation

Vacation, soothes our minds and thoughts. It signifies a bunch of feelings that include relaxation, calmness, adventure and energy altogether! So, vacation is our time, just our time with ourselves and our loved ones!

Now, let's try to figure out that is vacation same for each one of us? Why are vacations important? What if we don't have or what if don't go on a vacation?

A sentence is said to be complete, only when it ends with a full stop. Expressive sentences end up with exclamation and interrogations end with a question mark. Punctuations decorate texts such that the reader finds it easier to interpret.

The point to state this here is that we all have different sorts of situations in our lives. But, in order to balance everything well, we need to think, reflect and live. Vacations gift us those precious moments to reflect, from what we regularly deflect, and that is nothing other than, we, ourselves! Rest is necessary for all, as it is a penultimate rule of our nature. So, it is critical to rest whenever possible, and to get ready to give our best. This rest, is vacation!

It is not mandatory to always go out somewhere on a vacation. A vacation just demands our time, for ourself, mostly with the people with whom we want to spend it altogether. A pause is necessary to reload ourselves, refill ourselves, and that is what a vacation actually initiates. So, a vacation acts as a catalyst to increase productivity and enhance satisfaction.

I would like to explain this more in detail, by means of a wordplay from my side -

Tu tham jaa
Kisi chhorr par...
Thaamkar khudko...

Waqt ki...
Baagdor ko!

Aakhir kitna daudega tu?
Thoda theher kar,
Thoda sambhal kar,
Phir jaana bhaagne...
Manzil teri hi hain...
Bas tujhe usee paane ki deri hain!

Main yeh nahi keh raha ki
Sab kuch chhodkar,
Bas tu aaraam kar...

Ha par bohat saara kaam,
Achhe se karne ke liye...
Tu thoda bohat aaraam bhi kar!

Sehat sambhaal,
Apnon ko waqt de...
Khudko sudhaar,
Aur kabhi ji le, apne liye!

Khudko jaan aur pehachaan...
Aur kama sammaan...

Zara waqt ko bhi toh mehasoos kara...
Ki woh tera hain!
Ki tu uska hain!

Uss ghadi ko bhi toh yaad dila de...
Ki kuch samay ke liye...
Vo tere ishaaro par chale!

Har kacchvaa hamesha nahi jeetta...
Aur har khargosh,
Hamesha nahi haarta.

Teri kahani hain...
Isliye tu khudko samajh...
Aur jab jaha mumkin ho...
Avkaash le!

Every person has a different story, and so, a vacation is not similar for all of us. But there are still some common facts about vacations. Yes, vacations make us happy, we are free to live our way, without any restrictions, and so, they are important!

If you don't have a regular vacation, you are not in a great condition. Rather I would say, you're not living your life to its fullest! Modern work life balance is difficult to attain with these evolving times, but it is crucial for overall life satisfaction and growth.

Vacations give us an opportunity, to meet our closed ones, get in touch with new people, wander around, learn new things, experiment, relax, enjoy and reflect! I'm about to get my vacation soon. What about you mate?

I can just say, take a break and vacate yourself, whenever and wherever possible, because after every busy day, there is a night to rest!

CHAPTER VIII

Festivals

"A festival is one that brings everyone together,
A festival is one that connects minds and hearts to each other."

According to Wikipedia, a festival is a day or time when people celebrate something, especially a religious event. Another popular thesaurus meaning of a festival, is a series of plays, films, musical performances, etc. often held regularly at a place. So, on referring the above definitions, we conclude, that festivals bring people together! They bind communities, with humanity and thoughtfulncss!

Cultural festivals, sports festival, technical festivals, etc. are some diversified versions of the varied festivals that are celebrated everywhere. In addition to these are the college festivals, department festivals, institutional festivals, organisational celebrations, the district, the state, the national and the international festivals, etc.

On referring the above list, we understand that we cannot count the total number of festivals that are celebrated across different geographies! Practically, it is a difficult task to list down all of them! Each festival has its distinct features and characteristics, origins, support, faith, related factors, etc.

I am fortunate enough to be an Indian, as we celebrate diverse festivals unitedly, throughout the year!

Below is my wordplay on Festivals -

"Aksar hum sab,
Saath milkar,
Tyohaar manaate hain!
Ek dusre sang,
Khushi-gumm baatkar,
Bhaichaara badhaate hain!

Har tyohaar,
Apne aap mein ek paheli hain!
Bilkul waise hi, jaise,
Krishna ki Radha saheli hain!

Inn tyohaaron ke maadhyam se,
Hum ek hote hain!
Insaaniyat ki fasal,
Hum sab saath jote hain!

Kaafi arse baad milkar,
Kuch ashq bahaate hain,
Bane-bigde naaton ko,
Dil se milaate hain!

Rozmarra ki bhaagdaud se,
Inn tyohaaron ki wajah se hi,
Hum shayad,
Apne liye,
Kuch pal jutaate hain!
Kuch pal churaate hain!
Kuch pal jeete hain!"

Kindly read the part below carefully -

"Toh kya hua,
Agar pehle jaise hum tyohaar
Offline nahi manaate hain?

Online hi sahi,
Kam se kam,
Apnon se,
Hum internet ke zariye,
Mukhaatib toh hote hain!

Pehle baat palon ko saath jeene ki thi,
Ab shayad ek dusre ke status mein hone ki hain!

Agar kabhi galti se,
Kahi koi apna dikh bhi jaata hain,
Toh bhi hum ek dusre ko pehachan nahi paate,
Pehle jaise khulkar baatein nahi kar paate!

Pata hain kyu?
Kyunki, pehle jaisa apna offline network ab raha nahi,
Sab kuch, online jo ho gaya hain!

Ab iss online-offline ke chakkar mein,
Hum shayad tyohaaron ke mukhya uddeshya ko hi bhoolte jaa rahe hain!

Vo uddeshya kya hain,
Iska jawaab maine iss poori peshkash mein kai baar diya hain!

Chunna hume hain,
Online, ya Offline!"

With this, I would like to wrap up for this one! Celebrate festivals sustainably by binding communities and prospering ahead together!

CHAPTER IX

Happiness

I know that all of us know, what Happiness means! Rather I must say, we have felt and experienced it sometime or the other. 'Happiness', the word itself is an enigma of positive vibes! It is something, that we all need in our lives!

No one in this world, likes to be sad. Our circumstances, situations and shortcomings bend our happiness into sadness. A smile on one's face, instead of going upwards, goes downwards, leading to negative vibes. This is sadness!

Now the question arises, why is it that our life has these positive and negative vibes? Can a person not be happy always?

There is only a single word answer to these queries. Now you must be thinking, what is it, as how can only a single word solve these giant qualitative questions!

The answer is 'Balance'!

Like every coin has a head and a tail, same applies to us! We've Happiness and Sadness as the two sides of our individual life-coin!

Happiness can be further classified into some types. The two most noteworthy types include Self Happiness and Collective Happiness. As their names specifically point out, self happiness means the happiness gained in our favour, then might it be in the favour of the rest, or not! While collective happiness can be defined as the happiness gained by the community, for the community and is of the community! It might or might not have any selfish gains, and collective happiness caters the development of any society, by promoting the right, almost every time!

The smile on a mother's face, when her child is happy, is a form of happiness, that cannot be word-framed.

The satisfaction on a father's face, when his child attains something good, is again noteworthy, as even it is a great example of happiness!

The shine in a teacher's eyes, when his or her student achieves something worth, is also happiness!

Our world is full of pleasures and pains! Not all pains are bad, and not all pleasures are good! Both of these are important in our lives, as the balance between these, according to me, is Life!

I genuinely feel, my lines below, will help you decode, what exactly is Happiness -

Sachhi khushi vo nahi,
Jo kisi se kuch cheenkar mili ho,
Sachhi khushi toh vo hain,
Jo uss kuch ko jeetkar mili ho!

Sachhi hasi vo nahi,
Jo dard bhari ho,
Sachhi hasi toh woh hain,
Jo saare dard bhulakar aayi ho!

Sachhi dhadkan vo nahi,
Jo sirf dhadak kar guzri ho,
Sachhi dhadkan toh vo hain,
Jo humne jeekar guzaari ho!

Sachhi aahat vo nahi,
Jo kisi ke aane ya jaane se hui ho,
Sachhi aahat toh vo hain,
Jo mehasoos ki gayi ho!

Aur...
Sachhi ibadat vo nahi..
Jo kisi ko batakar ki gayi ho,
Sachhi ibadat toh vo hain,

Jo sirf khudko pata ho,
Aur kisi ko nahi!

With this take on Happiness, before winding up, I would like to say that -

Whenever I write,
I gain happiness!

Whenever I edit,
I gain happiness!

Whenever I talk, compose, act, create, and motivate,
I gain happiness!

I take up everything with energy,
With a spirit and attitude of lifelong learning!

Time has made me understand that experience is happiness, and consistent practice is a bridge to excellence!

Ultimately, I can say that...
I gain happiness,
From everything that I do!

I've learnt to be happy,
What about you, my friend?

Take a moment, reflect about it and be happy!

CHAPTER X

Truth

A fact can either be a reality, or a work of fiction. Whatever we see or hear, can have multiple sides, and can showcase a variety of outcomes, according to different situations, timeframes, people and things present there.

Precision with clarity in life is necessary, as even slight negligence, can lead to misunderstandings, problems, fights, etc. Honesty, better known as a jewel of a person's character, plays a critical role everywhere.

According to my evaluation, we all have our truths, and we're the only ones, who know them all! So, truth is mysterious!

A fact or belief that is accepted to be true, is truth! The quality or state of being true, is truth! Anything that is true, or is in accordance with the fact or reality, is truth! But let's not just stick only to these definitions! Let's explore truth in depth, together!

A popular English quote says -
"Three things cannot be long hidden: the sun, the moon, and the truth!"

Another one points out that -
"Wisdom is found, only in truth!"

My understanding about the same states -
"Denying truth, does not change the facts!"

As always, here's a wordplay on "Truth" -

"Sach sirf vo nahi hain,
Jo aakhon ko nazar aaye,
Kahi ya kisi se suna jaaye!

Sach toh vo hain,
Jo dil aur dimaag,

Dono maan jaaye!

Sachhai baaton se baya nahi hoti...
Sachhai toh iraadon aur
Faislon se quayam hoti hain!

Jhoot hamesha bura nahi hota...
Aur sach hamesha kadva nahi hota!

Sachhai chupana,
Kabhi kabhi zaroori hota hain!

Par iska yeh matlab nahi,
Ki sach hamesha ke liye chup jaayega!

Sach ki sachhai,
Mann ki, dil ki aur
Niyat ki buniyaad hoti hain!

Jhoot aasaani se bikta hain,
Isiliye hum kai baar
Sach ko nazarandaaz kar dete hain!

Duniya jo dikhaati hain...
Vo hamesha sach nahi...
Baatein jo sunaati hain...
Vo hamesha sach nahi...
Aur hamari aakhein jo bataati hain...
Vo bhi hamesha sach nahi!

Sach toh vo hain...
Jo hame hamara nazariya, tajurba aur
Hamari galtiyaan sikhati hain!

Zindagi ke pal, rishton ki dorr,
Aur ruhh ki achaai manaati hain!
Sachhai ka taaj jiske sar aaya...
Quaynaat se usne

Beshumaar pyar hain paaya!

Sachaai ki raah par,
Mushkilon ka aana-jaana toh laga rehata hain...

Par jo datkar...
Sach ka saath deta hain,
Sach bhi usi ki zindagi ka savera banta hain!

Sachhai ka saath dekar toh dekh lo...
Sukoon mehasoos hota hain...
Kaafi achha lagta hain!"

I hope, this described Truth, to its best, to its fullest!

Personally, I feel, this topic Truth has multiple dimensions to cover, and I have sincerely tried to touch and express most of those here, bit by bit!

Epilogue

We all are here to figure out what we are, who we are, why we are alive and till when, we'll be active in this world. It's okay to admit that we don't know everything. Life is all about living, experiencing, exploring and learning.

Set your mind to think in a certain way to be creative. Think outside the boundary of being reasonable. We all can harness that ability to think and innovate. So, trigger your thoughts, don't just complain always. Try to make the most out of what you have and most importantly, be humble and practical!

Value all things and people, as interest matters to generate interests. If you've to pretend to be someone else than your original self, just to be somewhere, or to be with someone, then probably, you don't belong there. Be authentic, be you!

Communication is the true oxygen of any relationship! If you feel things are not going well, sit, reflect, communicate with people and try to resolve those shortcomings. Time moves at a constant rate, so does our life. Nothing stays forever, so live the moments that you have, with your loved ones, with those deserving ones who care for you, who respect you and your existence! Cherish what you have!

Bring value addition to the community, utilize your time in good activities. Determine opportunities, seize those! Luck is a result-oriented synonym of consistently directed efforts.

In every moment of our life, we are losing and gaining some or the other thing. Attitude is more important than aptitude. So, prioritise well, organise, manage your story and yes, be quick, life is unpredictable! Choose wisely and be a successful outcome of your own decisions!

Leave your comfort zone and serve quality! It is not important how much you work because how well you work counts more! Be a problem solver. Perform in adversities. Stick to your passion and inspire to live! Practice regularly to be the best! Learn from people around, as each one of us has a different story. Timing matters, so does talent and dedication. Be the protagonist of your life.

Failed? It's okay, don't lose hope! Rise again, face it again! We all can do wonders! So, Try! Experiment! Learn and Win!

With these words of wisdom, I would like to halt here for now.

I humbly request you,
to tell me the Truth,
whether "Decoding Zindagi",
met your expectations or not!

Genuine feedbacks are heartily welcomed,
As I strongly believe -
"There is always a room for improvisation!"

Just don't hesitate to tell me the Truth!
I respect you, and your truthfulness!

Hope to hear from you, soon!

"Decoding Zindagi" will definitely continue ahead for sure, together!

Thank You!!

9 798885 694711

Printed by Libri Plureos GmbH in Hamburg, Germany